This book belongs to

....

Written by Rosie Greening.
Illustrated by Stuart Lynch.

Groovicorns in the City

Rosie Greening • Stuart Lynch

make believe ideas

In far-off Funky Forest
lived a friendly dancing crew

who were WAY more cool than unicorns

(and much politer, too!)

Psst . . . sometimes I'm cool!

This group was called the
GROOVICORNS,
and when you saw their moves,
you couldn't help but join the fun
and get into the groove!

One sunny day, an **acorn** note
came for the dancing troop,
from a **squirrel** in the city
who knew the **groovy** group.

Squirrel's Treehouse
Central Park
Moanhattan

Dear groovicorns,

Moanhattan needs your dancing:
everyone is GLUM.
Please come to the city
and help them all have fun!

Love Squirrel xxx

"It won't take long!" cried out the group.

LET'S DANCE!

"We'll **cheer** them with our **dancing**,

TV GUIDE

and hopefully be **back** in time to watch Strictly Come Prancing!"

S.S. Groove

Moanhattan City

They left their Funky Forest friends
and jumped on board a ferry.
They were off to help out Squirrel
and to make Moanhattan merry!

Beep! Beep! Beep! Beep!

The worst bit was the gloomycorns, who acted like machines.

They never smiled . . . .

or said hello . . . .

. . . they just stared at their screens!

"They're so **gloomy!**" Ziggy cried.
"We **don't** stand a chance."

But Roxy said,
"We have to **try:** come on,
it's time to **dance!**"

They found a square with **glaring screens**
all going **flicker-flash**.

WIFI!

MORE DATA

MANE SQUARE

MOVIES

They took a **breath**,
cried, **"6, 7, 8 . . ."**
and then **began** to . . .

The gloomycorns **bumped** into them, **distracted** by their phones. "They won't **look up!**" cried Ziggy, with a **big**, un-groovy groan.

They went down to the subway, where the gloomycorns looked bored.
But with all the screens and headphones, every dance move was ignored!

They breakdanced,

flossed

and did the dab,

but no routine would do.
The gloomycorns were in the cloud,
and nothing could get through.

"This is hopeless!" cried the group.
"Those screens are all they see."

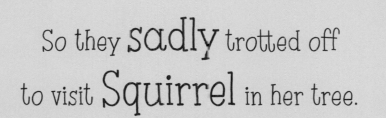

So they sadly trotted off
to visit Squirrel in her tree.

Moanhattan
Park

Squirrel said, "Don't worry, guys –
you tried your **best**, I know.
Could you **teach me** some dance moves
before you have to go?"

So the groovicorns **explained** their **steps**, and Squirrel had such **fun**, that she **filmed** them on her **acorn** phone ...

Step left...turn around...
hands in the air...
step right...star jump!

...to **watch** once they were done.

When they watched the **video**,
it filled them all with **cheer**.
It was **happy, fun** and **colourful**
and gave them an **idea** . . .

They posted it on HoofTube
and as **quickly** as can be,

it appeared on **every screen**
for **all** the gloomycorns to see!

All across the city, everybody learnt the moves, and the gloomycorns put down their phones to get into the groove.

There was **singing** in the subways . . .

. . . and **Swirling** in the street.

The gloomycorns were having **fun** and **dancing** to the beat!

After that, Moanhattan shone with laughter, life and colour, as the gloomycorns all learnt to laugh and talk to one another.

And **back at home**, the groovicorns were keeping **busy**, too.

They were **filming** groovy **dances** . . .

...for EVERYONE to do!